Me and My Dragon

SCARED OF HALLOWEEN

David Biedrzycki

 Charlesbridge

Published by Charlesbridge
85 Main Street
Watertown, MA 02472
(617) 926-0329
www.charlesbridge.com

Library of Congress Cataloging-in-Publication Data
Biedrzycki, David.
    Me and my dragon: scared of Halloween / David Biedrzycki.
        p. cm.
    Summary: A boy tries to find the perfect Halloween costume for his pet dragon,
so they can go trick-or-treating together.
    ISBN 978-1-58089-658-0 (reinforced for library use)
    ISBN 978-1-58089-659-7 (softcover)
    ISBN 978-1-60734-608-1 (ebook)
1. Halloween—Juvenile fiction. 2. Dragons—Juvenile fiction.
3. Pets—Juvenile fiction. 4. Halloween costumes—
Juvenile fiction. I. Title. II. Title: Scared
of Halloween.
PZ7.B4745Mg 2013
[E]—dc23   2012024438

Printed in Singapore
(hc) 10 9 8 7 6 5 4 3 2 1
(sc) 10 9 8 7 6 5 4 3 2 1

Illustrations done in Adobe Photoshop
Display type set in Jellybest by Jakob Fischer at
    www.pizzadude.dk
Text type set in Providence Sans by Guy Jeffrey
    Nelson, FontShop International
Color separations by KHL Chroma Graphics, Singapore
Printed and bound February 2013 by Imago in Singapore
Production supervision by Brian G. Walker
Designed by Diane M. Earley

To my friend Jim James and
Park St. Books in Medfield, MA—
the best children's bookstore EVER!

Me and my dragon like
all the same things.
We love birthday parties.

We're crazy
about parades.

Fireworks dazzle us.

We enjoy the same stuff—
except for trick-or-treating.

I love Halloween.

Poor Dragon.
I explained to him that mummies,
zombies, and werewolves aren't real.

But he was still scared.

I thought that if I made Dragon a costume, he would understand what Halloween is all about.

101 COSTUMES FOR PETS

Dad did not like the mummy idea.

Robodragon
almost had
a major
malfunction.

The werewolf costume looked fantastic, but Dragon couldn't howl.

OOOOOOOOOEEEWWAAaa

The zombie costume
almost scared Dragon
to death. Yikes!

The tutu was cute.
Too bad it was flammable.

I had my costume all ready.
I was going to go as Elvis.

But then Dragon stole the show.
No way was that going to work.
Everyone knows there's only
one Elvis.

Dragon was sad because he didn't have a costume. I tried to make him feel better by reading him our favorite book.

That gave
Dragon an idea.

We were ready just in time. We flew
off and went from house to house.

Everyone loved Dragon's costume.

We came home with a pile of candy
and started counting it all.
I put Dragon in charge of guarding it.

Now we both love Halloween!